"**I could have sworn I left my papers on my desk.** They were all in a red folder. But the folder's not there now," Mrs. Simpson told Titus, Timothy, and Sarah-Jane.

"Your door is wide open," Titus said as they got off the elevator and walked down the hall.

"It's because of the paint fumes," explained Mrs. Simpson.

The cousins edged their way in and looked around. There were drop cloths over everything. The apartment looked more like the South Pole than a place where someone lived. They had tackled tough cases before, but this!

Would it be *too* tough for the T.C.D.C.?

Solve all the Beatitudes Mysteries along with Sarah-Jane, Ti, and Tim:

THE MYSTERY OF THE
DISAPPEARING
PAPERS

Elspeth Campbell Murphy
Illustrated by Chris Wold Dyrud

Chariot Books™
David C. Cook Publishing Co.

A Wise Owl Book
Published by Chariot Books™,
an imprint of David C. Cook Publishing Co.
David C. Cook Publishing Co., Elgin, Illinois 60120
David C. Cook Publishing Co., Weston, Ontario

THE MYSTERY OF THE DISAPPEARING PAPERS
© 1989 by Elspeth Campbell Murphy for text and Chris Wold Dyrud
for illustrations

Cover design by Steve Smith
First printing, 1989
Printed in the United States of America
94 93 92 91   5 4

Library of Congress Cataloging-in-Publication Data
Murphy, Elspeth Campbell.
   The mystery of the disappearing papers / Elspeth Campbell Murphy;
illustrated by Chris Wold Dyrud.
      p. cm.—(The Beatitudes mysteries)
   "A Wise owl book."—T.p. verso.
   Summary; Three cousins investigate the disappearance of a college
student's research paper and learn the meaning of "Blessed are the
pure in heart."
   ISBN 1-55513-576-5
   [1. Cousins—Fiction. 2. Mystery and detective stories.
3. Beatitudes—Fiction.] I. Dyrud, Chris Wold, ill. II. Title.
III. Series: Murphy, Elspeth Campbell. Beatitudes mysteries.
PZ7.M95316Myam   1989
[Fic]—19   89-31260
                                                       CIP
                                                        AC

CONTENTS

"Blessed are the pure in heart,
for they will see God."

Matthew 5:8 (NIV)

1
A BOOMING BUSINESS

Titus McKay was one of the busiest people in his whole apartment building.

As word spread throughout the Dolphin Towers about how dependable he was, more and more people had started hiring him. They hired him after school and on weekends to do odd jobs and run errands. And because Titus would *go for* this and *go for* that, he was known as a "gofer."

Titus had just taken coffee and donuts to some people next door to him on the nineteenth floor. Now he was on his way back down in the elevator to get a donut for himself.

He was glad his gofer business was booming, but he was also looking forward to taking things easy today. His two cousins, Timothy Dawson and Sarah-Jane Cooper, were in the city for the weekend. And right now they were waiting for him in the new little donut shop next door. The shop was very convenient, because its back door opened onto the main lobby of the Dolphin Towers apartment building.

Titus thought the donut shop was just about the coziest place in the whole world. Outside it might be a blustery, gray November morning, but inside it was all warm, delicious smells and red-checked tablecloths.

Certainly his cousins looked cozy where they sat in the corner with Titus's father. All three of them were completely absorbed in what they were doing.

Titus's father, who taught at the university, was going over some lecture notes.

Timothy was carefully picking off microscopic pieces of coconut from his donut. It wasn't a coconut donut, but it had been sitting *next* to a coconut donut on the tray. And Timothy wasn't taking any chances.

Sarah-Jane was studying a jewelry catalog. Sarah-Jane was nutty about catalogs anyway,

8

but she was particularly fascinated by this one. All three families were going together to get the cousins' grandmother a special ring for Christmas. It would have a birthstone for each grandchild in it. (That would be four, counting Timothy's baby sister, Priscilla.) Sarah-Jane practically had the whole birthstone chart in the catalog memorized.

Titus went to the counter to get his donut. At the same time, a good-looking young man, a graduate student, came in through the back door. "Titus, my man," he said cheerfully.

Then to Titus's father he said, "Good morning, Professor McKay. Congratulate me!" He looked so pleased with himself, you'd have thought his sleek, leather briefcase was filled with birthstones.

"Oh, hello, Brad," said Titus's father. "You're looking chipper this morning. What happened? Is your research paper going better? Have you finally settled on a subject for it?"

"Yes, Sir, I have. I really feel that I've made a major breakthrough. I can't wait to tell my adviser about it. You know, he's been after me, because I've gotten a little behind."

Titus's father raised his eyebrows, and Brad turned a little red. "Uh—well," he corrected himself. "I mean, he was after me because I hadn't actually *started*. But I'm all set now. My aunt is still off traveling somewhere, so I have the apartment all to myself. I just came down for a coffee break. Then it's right back upstairs and back to work." He turned to Titus. "How's the gofer business, kiddo?"

"Busy," said Titus. "But I'm taking it easy today."

Titus was just about to introduce his cousins to Brad, when the lobby door burst open and a flustered, middle-aged lady rushed in. "Oh, Titus! Thank goodness I've found you! Your mother said you would be here. I need your help. I think I'm losing my mind!"

2
THE SCATTERBRAIN

Neither Titus nor his father got too excited by this outburst, since Mrs. Simpson lost her mind at least two or three times a week.

Mrs. Simpson was a graduate student in history, the same as Brad. Professor McKay was her faculty adviser. Titus's father always said he didn't know how Helen Simpson could be so brilliant and so scatterbrained all at the same time. She was always hiring Titus to help her out.

"Oh, Dr. McKay! Oh, Titus! I've really done it this time! Somehow I've misplaced my *entire research paper*! All my notes. My outline. The beginnings of a rough draft . . ."

"Bummer," said Brad sympathetically.

"Well, it's my own fault," groaned Mrs.

Simpson. "My apartment is in *complete chaos*!"

Brad nodded. "Because of the painters, you mean."

"Well, I'm just losing my mind, that's all there is to it," declared Mrs. Simpson.

The cousins looked at one another and smiled. Mrs. Simpson might be scatterbrained. But she was also sweet and funny.

"Whatever possessed me to get my apartment painted the same time I'm trying to write the most important paper of my life? I ask you. I thought I was so organized, getting the apartment painted well before Christmas. Ohhh!" She groaned and put her head in her hands. "I need my gofer. Titus, will you come and help me look?"

Beneath all the exaggerated talk, Titus could tell that Mrs. Simpson was truly anxious. He glanced at his cousins and said, "I can give you something better than a gofer, Mrs. Simpson. I can give you the T.C.D.C."

"It sounds wonderful," said Mrs. Simpson. "But what's a 'teesy-deesy'?"

"It's letters," explained Titus.

"Capital T.

Capital C.

Capital D.

Capital C.

It stands for the Three Cousins Detective Club." And he introduced Timothy and Sarah-Jane.

Brad chuckled. "Detectives, huh? That's cute. Well, I've got to shove off. Loads of work to do. Helen—take care. I hope you find your paper real soon. Bye, all."

"*Cute!*" muttered Timothy when Brad had gone. "We're not *cute!*"

"No, of course you're not," said Mrs. Simpson quietly. "You're serious workers, and I need some serious help."

It was true that Mrs. Simpson sometimes exaggerated. But she hadn't exaggerated very much when she had said her apartment was in complete chaos.

"Your door is wide open," Titus said as they got off the elevator on the sixteenth floor and walked down the hall.

"It's because of those awful paint fumes," explained Mrs. Simpson. "Besides, I've been in and out all morning with laundry and whatnot. So it just seemed easier to prop the door open. Watch your step."

The cousins edged their way in and looked around. They had tackled tough cases before, but this—! There were drop cloths over everything. The whole apartment looked more like

the South Pole than a place where someone lived.

So much for taking it easy, thought Titus.

Mrs. Simpson said, "I could have sworn I left my papers on my desk. They were all in a red, expandable folder. But the folder's not there now."

To prove it, she lifted the drop cloth covering her desk, and the detective-cousins stepped over to take a peek.

"But you don't always work at your desk, right?" asked Titus.

Mrs. Simpson sighed and looked around. "No, you're right, Titus. Sometimes I work at the dining room table. Or sitting up in bed. Or lying on the sofa. Or even standing up at the kitchen counter."

The cousins glanced at one another in dismay. They were going to have to search the whole apartment.

They started in the little office. They checked the desk again (just to make doubly sure) and lifted up the drop cloths on chairs and shelves. From the office, they moved on to other rooms. It was super-hard work. That was because they had to be super-careful not to step in paint cans or brush up against walls.

It was also super-discouraging, because they didn't find the red folder.

Also, the paint smell was beginning to make them feel a little sick.

Mrs. Simpson said, "I'm more used to the smell, so I'll keep working here. But why don't you kids go take a little break?"

Then Titus thought of a way they could take a break from the paint and still keep working.

"Maybe you left your notes in the laundry room," he suggested. "We could check there."

Mrs. Simpson agreed that this was a good idea. So the cousins headed downstairs on the elevator.

Sarah-Jane said, "Mrs. Simpson is very nice, but she really is absentminded."

"I guess so," said Titus. "But I always thought that was mostly just the way she talked. I never thought she could really lose her folder like this."

Timothy said, "But it's not really *lost,* is it? I mean, if it's not in the laundry room, then it's still got to be in her apartment, right?"

"I guess so," said Titus. But it still didn't make sense.

4
MUNCHKINS?!?

The cousins decided they needed a breath of fresh air, so they rode down to the lobby and went out the revolving door. And right back in—it was cold out there!

As they came rushing past, Will, the doorman, called out to them that he needed a gofer.

"I need to find Brad Taylor," he explained. "His aunt just called me from the airport. She wanted me to give him the message that she's coming back this afternoon to stay for a few days before she leaves again."

That surprised them. Not that Miss Taylor was coming back for a few days, but that she couldn't reach her nephew to tell him.

Titus asked, "Why couldn't Miss Taylor get ahold of Brad on the phone? He's up in their apartment right now. He's working on his research paper.''

"Yes," said Sarah-Jane. "He just came down a little while ago for a coffee break—"

"And then he was going right back upstairs," finished Timothy. "I don't get it."

"I don't get it, either," said Will. "I haven't seen him go out. But his aunt can't reach him, and neither can I."

"We'll keep an eye out for him," said Titus.

So much for taking things easy. Now they had two things to look for: the red folder and Brad Taylor.

They didn't find either one in the laundry room.

Titus said, "Sometimes Mrs. Simpson rides the exercise bike in the exercise room. It's right next door to the laundry room. People can put a book on the handlebars and read while they're pedaling. So—maybe she had her notes in there."

They went to check.

They didn't find the red folder, but they did find Brad. He was lifting weights and admiring

himself in the mirror. He grinned at them. "Hi, munchkins. What's up?"

Sarah-Jane put her hands on her hips. "What are you doing here?" she snapped. "You're supposed to be upstairs working on your paper!"

Timothy and Titus glanced at each other. Apparently Sarah-Jane didn't like being thought of as a cute little munchkin any more than they did.

But Brad just laughed. "I'm taking a break, OK? No crime in that, is there? By the way, how's the detective business going?"

"Not so bad," said Timothy. "We found *you,* didn't we?"

"Me? Why were you looking for me?"

Titus explained. "Your aunt has been trying to get ahold of you. She left a message with Will, the doorman, because she couldn't get an answer on your phone. And Will sent us to find you."

"Oh, yeah?" said Brad, going back to his weights. "Well, you found me. What's the message?"

Titus said, "She's coming back for a few days before she leaves on another trip. She'll be here in a little while."

Instantly Brad's carefree manner vanished.

"Oh, no!" he cried, snatching up his gym bag. "Gotta go. Gotta get back upstairs. Catch you later, munchkins."

And with that he was gone.

"What was *that* all about?" asked Timothy.

"Yeah," added Sarah-Jane. "Brad sure didn't seem very happy about his aunt coming back. What's the matter? Doesn't he like her?"

"I don't know," said Titus thoughtfully. "*I* think she's really nice. And she's a friend of Mrs. Simpson's, too. Mrs. Simpson always teases her. She says, 'Doris, you travel all over the world, trying to find someone nosier than you are.' And Miss Taylor always laughs and says, 'Helen, I have a lively curiosity, that's all.'

"But it's true—Miss Taylor is always asking questions. She notices *everything*. Maybe that drives Brad crazy, I don't know. But anyway, he's lucky she lets him use her apartment. They're on the eighth floor."

Sarah-Jane said, "Maybe Brad left the apartment in a mess. Maybe that's why he took off like that. He has to get the apartment cleaned up before his aunt sees it."

"Maybe," said Timothy. "But I don't know about Brad. . . ."

Titus pretended to be shocked. "What's the matter, Tim? Don't you *like* being called a cute-little-kiddo-detective-munchkin?"

Timothy laughed. "That's exactly what I mean!" Then he struggled to explain it better. "It's like Brad is trying to be friendly and all, but I don't think he really wants to."

Sarah-Jane nodded. "He thinks he's *so cool.*"

"The original Mr. Cool," agreed Titus. "Cooler than everybody else."

"That's what I mean," said Timothy. "I get the feeling that he thinks everybody else is really dumb. So, inside, it's like he's laughing at everybody. But, outside, he still tries to act like a nice guy. It's as if—the way he's trying to be on the *outside* and the way he really thinks on the *inside* don't match up."

Titus and Sarah-Jane nodded without saying anything. They understood what Timothy meant about Brad, but they didn't exactly know how to explain it, either.

And that still didn't explain why he had rushed off to the apartment when he heard his aunt was coming home.

They got even more confused when Brad showed up at Titus's apartment a little while later. The cousins had told Mrs. Simpson they would be back to help her look for her folder again after lunch. They were just getting ready to leave when Brad came to the door. He said, "Oh, wow. I'm glad I caught you. I have this *really important,* sort-of detective job. I need to hire you."

6
THE BEAUTIFUL BIRTHDAY GIFT

Titus wondered if he had heard right. *Brad* wanted to hire *munchkins*? But before he could ask any questions, Brad held out a beautifully wrapped birthday gift.

The cousins glanced at one another. What was going on? Whose birthday was it?

Brad said with an embarrassed little laugh, "Hey. I bet you kids wondered why I ran off like that. But I can explain. See, the thing is, it's my aunt's birthday next week. And I got her this really terrific present. But she's—I don't know how to explain this to you—she's a great lady and everything—but she's a—a—"

Titus helped him out. "A snoop?"

Brad looked startled. "You don't miss much, do you?"

Titus just shrugged.

"Anyway," Brad continued. "I looked all over my apartment for a good hiding place, but I couldn't come up with one."

Sarah-Jane said, "So you want us to hold onto the present for you. If we keep it here, in Titus's apartment, there's no chance your aunt will find it."

Brad looked enormously relieved. "Oh, wow. *Could* you? That would be so great."

"Sure," said Timothy matter-of-factly. "No problem."

"Great!" said Brad. "Oh! One more thing. Let's keep this *top secret,* OK, bambinos? Not a world to Helen Simpson, because she'll just tell my aunt."

The cousins patiently assured him that his secret was safe with them.

Brad gave them a long, sincere, serious look. "Hey. Thanks, kiddos."

Holding onto a birthday present was not the hardest job in the world.

The cousins didn't even have to hide it,

because Miss Taylor probably wouldn't be in Titus's apartment. But they decided to play it safe. After all, Miss Taylor knew her own birthday was coming up next week. So if she *did* come to Titus's apartment and saw the present, she would be sure to ask who it was for and what was in it. And, of course, they wouldn't want to lie.

Hiding a birthday present was not the hardest job in the world, either.

At least, it wasn't hard for the T.C.D.C. They were excellent at hiding things. Of course, sometimes that was a problem. Once, they were in charge of hiding the Easter eggs for a preschool party. They did the job so well, none of the little kids could find any eggs, and they all started crying. So the cousins had to help hunt for their own eggs. And even *they* couldn't find the last one. At least not until a l-o-n-g time later, when the smell gave it away.

The three cousins talked about a lot of different places to hide Brad's present for his aunt. But they finally decided to put it in the hall closet where Titus's mother kept wrapping

paper and bows. That way, the present just kind of blended right in.

"EX-cellent," said Titus.

"Neat-O," said Timothy.

"So cool," said Sarah-Jane.

They knew they were probably congratulating themselves too much for something that wasn't *that* big a deal. But they were trying to make up for how they felt about Mrs. Simpson's red folder.

Not good.

So far, it seemed they were doing a lot better

with hiding birthday gifts than finding research papers.

It was time to go back to Mrs. Simpson's apartment and start looking all over again.

7

BRIGHT-EYED AND BUSHY-TAILED

The cousins found Mrs. Simpson and her friend Miss Taylor, Brad's aunt, sitting in the middle of the lumpy living room. They were waiting for the coffee to brew in the lumpy kitchen. It was hard to tell how Mrs. Simpson was feeling. On the one hand, she seemed glad to be chatting with her old friend. But on the other hand, she seemed more depressed than ever about her missing research paper.

Mrs. Simpson introduced Timothy and Sarah-Jane to Miss Taylor, who immediately wanted to know all about them.

She was small and plump and so full of energy that she always reminded Titus of a squirrel. The description "bright-eyed and bushy-tailed" fit her better than anyone else

Titus had ever seen. Even her questions were lively. She wasn't a sneaky kind of nosy, Titus thought. She was just incredibly interested—in everything and everybody.

"Now, let's see if I've got this straight," Miss Taylor was saying. "Your last names are all different. Titus McKay, Timothy Dawson, and Sarah-Jane Cooper. Does this mean you're related on your mothers' side?"

"Yes," said Sarah-Jane, warming immediately to Miss Taylor. "Our mothers are sisters. My mother is Susan. Titus's mother is Jane. And Timothy's mother is Sarah. I'm named after both my aunts."

"How lovely!" cried Miss Taylor. "And are there any more cousins?"

"Yes!" replied Sarah-Jane, her enthusiasm growing. "Timothy has a baby sister named Priscilla. And she's the cutest, sweetest, cuddliest, little baby you ever saw. . . ."

Titus and Timothy looked at each other and groaned. Sarah-Jane was a little goofy when it came to babies—especially Priscilla. And Sarah-Jane was also a chatterbox—especially when she got around other chatterboxes, like Miss Taylor.

"And guess what!" Sarah-Jane continued. "We're all going together to get my grandmother this *beautiful* ring for Christmas. It's so cool! It will have four birthstones, one for each of us grandkids. Is that *your* birthstone?" she asked, pointing to a dainty ring on Miss Taylor's finger. "I love purple!"

Miss Taylor looked enormously pleased. "Yes, dear, so do I. That's why I'm lucky my birthstone is an amethyst."

All this talk about *birthstones* made Titus nervous. He was afraid something might slip out about Miss Taylor's *birthday* gift. He had to change the subject—fast. He noticed the painters had gone to lunch. So he said, "Mrs. Simpson, did you ask the painters about your missing papers?"

Mrs. Simpson smiled at him. But it was a sad kind of smile. "Oh, Titus. I've done everything I can think of. I asked the painters this morning if they'd seen the folder or moved it. But they hadn't. They were so busy painting, they didn't notice much of anything else."

Miss Taylor added brightly, "And then *I* questioned them again this afternoon."

Mrs. Simpson laughed. "You certainly did, Doris. But all you had to do was ask them if they'd seen the folder. You didn't have to ask them about their wives and children and their dreams for the future."

"We had a nice little chat," declared Miss Taylor. "At least the painters will talk to me. Not like that nephew of mine. He never tells me anything. Honestly, Helen, do you know what Brad's writing his paper on? You're both studying history. Maybe he talks to you."

But Mrs. Simpson just shook her head. "No. We got to talking on the elevator the other day, and I told him about my research. But he didn't say anything at all about his. I got the feeling it wasn't going too well."

Timothy piped up. "Brad told Uncle Richard this morning that he'd had a major breakthrough."

"Did he *indeed*?" asked Miss Taylor, looking more than ever like an alert, curious squirrel. "Now, that's odd. Because I didn't see any papers on his desk when I got home."

"Doris, you *didn't*!" cried Mrs. Simpson, truly shocked.

"Well . . . I did take just the *tiniest* peek around the apartment. But it doesn't really count as snooping, because I didn't find anything."

Mrs. Simpson just shook her head at this crazy logic.

But Titus was alarmed. "Don't tell me there are *two* missing papers now!"

"Yeah," said Timothy. "It's getting to be an epidemic."

Sarah-Jane had been unusually quiet for a long time, wearing a puzzled little frown. Now she suddenly jumped up, her eyes shining with excitement and cried, "Mrs. Simpson! Miss Taylor! Would you like some donuts to go with your coffee?"

8

THE CLUE IN THE CATALOG

Titus and Timothy waited until they were on the elevator before they burst out with:

"So what's going on, S-J?"

"Yeah, S-J. Why the sudden rush to the donut shop?"

(Mrs. Simpson and Miss Taylor had looked surprised—to say the least—when Sarah-Jane had suddenly suggested donuts. But the idea had appealed to them. So now the cousins were on their way down.)

Sarah-Jane gave the boys a triumphant smile. "We are going back to the donut shop, because, gentlemen, that's where I left my jewelry catalog."

Timothy buried his face in his hands. "I *don't believe* this!"

Titus clutched his hair in his fists. "Catalog! S-J, are you out of your mind? We're in the middle of an investigation. We still haven't found Mrs. Simpson's paper. And now maybe Brad's is missing, too. This is no time to be looking through catalogs."

Sarah-Jane laughed and hopped from one foot to the other. But all that she would say was, "Just wait."

Fortunately, the donut man had found her catalog and saved it for her at the counter. Sarah-Jane quickly flipped through the pages until she found exactly what she was looking for. It was the chart that showed which birthstone went with which month. She held the book out to Titus and Timothy. "There! I knew something was wrong."

The boys looked at the chart, but they didn't see what she was getting at.

"What month is it right now?" asked Sarah-Jane impatiently.

"November, of course. Why?"

"Look! Look! The birthstone for November is a *yellow topaz*!!"

"Yeah, so?"

Sarah-Jane looked like she was ready to scream. *"What color birthstone was Brad's aunt wearing?"*

"Purple," said Timothy.

"An amethyst," said Titus.

Suddenly the boys snatched the catalog out of Sarah-Jane's hands and examined the chart.

The purple amethyst was the birthstone for February.

9
THE PERFECT HIDING PLACE

They sank down on the little white chairs and looked at one another in a daze.

"I don't get it," said Timothy. "I mean, I do. But I don't. Miss Taylor's birthday is in February. I get that. But what I don't get is—why did Brad give us her birthday gift *today*? And why did he tell us her birthday was next week—when it's still November?"

"He lied," said Sarah-Jane simply.

"Yes, but why?"

They didn't have an answer to that.

Titus said, "I have the feeling Brad might have lied about something else, too."

Timothy and Sarah-Jane looked at him seriously, waiting for him to go on. Titus tried to explain.

"It's like Tim said before. Maybe Brad is different on the *inside* from how he tries to act on the *outside*. That made me think of when we were learning the Beatitudes in Sunday school. There's one that says, 'Blessed are the pure in heart, for they will see God.' My teacher said that people who are 'pure in heart' are honest all through. They're the same on the inside as on the outside. They don't lie to you. They don't try to trick people. And they don't try to get away with stuff—like cheating."

"So what's the other thing you think Brad lied about?" asked Timothy. "And how is he cheating?"

Titus took a deep breath. "OK. A university is like a school, right? Only harder. But Brad sure wasn't working hard on his paper today like he said he was going to. And he won't even tell his aunt what his paper is about. And she didn't find a paper when she looked through their apartment.

"I think we were wrong when we thought maybe Brad's paper was lost, too. I think Brad *never had a paper* in the first place. I think he lied when he said he had a major breakthrough on it."

Sarah-Jane said. "That makes sense. But then it doesn't make sense. Brad *has* to have a research paper. Otherwise, what is he going to show his adviser?"

Timothy said slowly, "Brad is going to show his adviser a paper, all right. But not his *own* paper. He's going to show him *Mrs. Simpson's* paper—and just say it's his. Cheating!"

Sarah-Jane gasped. "So—Mrs. Simpson didn't misplace her paper. She couldn't find it because Brad stole it. She's practically going out of her mind worrying about where it could be. And Brad has had it the whole time!"

Titus nodded. It was all coming together. "OK. Here's what probably happened. Maybe Brad went to talk to Mrs. Simpson about something this morning. And maybe he saw her leave her apartment, but she didn't see him. The door was wide open. So Brad saw his chance—and grabbed it. He snuck in past the painters. He found her folder on the desk in her office. That's where it made sense for the folder to be. Mrs. Simpson was sure she had left it there, and she was right the whole time."

Sarah-Jane nodded excitedly. "Brad must have been in her apartment—because, how else would he have known the painters were there? He said something about that this morning, remember?"

"You're absolutely right, S-J," said Titus. "How could he know? Brad lives on eight. And Mrs. Simpson lives on sixteen."

When Titus paused, Sarah-Jane took up the story. "So Brad put the folder in his briefcase and came down to the donut shop, where he saw all of us. He was so excited, because he figured his troubles were over. He couldn't resist bragging about his 'major breakthrough' and how he was just taking a break. But why would you take your *briefcase* on a *coffee break*?"

Then Timothy took up the story and told what he figured had happened next. "I bet Brad took the papers up to his apartment after that to look them over. But he didn't have to work hard on them, because Mrs. Simpson had already done all the work. So he figured he could just goof off in the exercise room. But then—he found out from us that his aunt was coming back when he didn't expect her. And he had to hide Mrs. Simpson's folder full of papers where his—um—curious aunt wouldn't find it."

Sarah-Jane sighed. "Well, Miss Taylor *didn't* find anything. So Brad must have put the missing papers in the perfect hiding place."

"Yes," said Titus softly. "That's *exactly* what he did. And I think I know where that is."

10
BETTER THAN DONUTS

"Are you sure we should do this?" asked Sarah-Jane nervously. "I mean, what if we're wrong? How can we wrap it up again so it doesn't show?"

"Don't look at me," said Timothy.

"It's a chance we have to take," said Titus firmly. "We'll just have to be super-careful, that's all."

The three were sitting in a circle on the floor of Titus's room with the beautiful birthday gift in the middle.

Slowly, carefully, Titus slid off the ribbon from one end and picked at the Scotch tape. When he got the paper partway undone, Timothy and Sarah-Jane held the wrapping, and Titus pulled out the box. It was like they were

pulling off a boot. Most of the wrapping was still in one piece.

Titus took a deep breath. "OK. Here goes." He lifted the lid off the box.

They didn't find a nice birthday present inside. But then—they hadn't expected to. Instead, they found exactly what they *had* expected: a red, expandable folder, stuffed with Helen Simpson's research paper.

Titus got his father and explained everything that had happened and all that they had figured out.

Professor McKay had that stiff look on his face he got only when he was really angry. But, of course, he wasn't angry at the cousins. It was simply that cheating always made him sick.

He said, "That young man. That Brad Taylor. He has always had everything he wanted. But then—when it came to something really hard, like this research paper—what does he do? He steals someone else's work and plans to pass it off as his own. The *deceit*!"

The cousins looked solemnly at one another. Brad was in major trouble.

Titus's father cleared his throat and said more cheerfully, "Well, now. Let's take this precious red folder down to Mrs. Simpson."

"There you are!" exclaimed Mrs. Simpson when she saw the cousins.

"Yes, where have you been?" asked Miss Taylor. "We've been waiting for our donuts."

The donuts! The cousins had forgotten all about them.

"Never mind," Titus's father said to Mrs. Simpson. "The T.C.D.C. has brought you something better than donuts."

And he held out the red folder.

Mrs. Simpson burst into tears. "Oh, thank you! This has been the most anxious day of my life. I've worked so hard on this paper. I couldn't bear to think that I was really scatter-brained enough to *lose* it!"

Miss Taylor said, "But more to the point, Helen, where did the children *find* it?"

So they told the whole story.

Titus had never seen an angry squirrel before. But looking at Miss Taylor, he knew he wouldn't want to tangle with one. Brad was in MAJOR trouble.

Mrs. Simpson had stopped crying. And now she said with a shaky little laugh, "Oh, dear. I don't quite know what to do next."

Titus had the answer. "Do what I'm going to do. Get a donut and take things easy!"

The End